FIVE PLACES YOU MEET FIFTEEN-YEAR-OLD YOU

ONE

Hell

"WELL, THIS IS NOT A SHOCK," SHE SAYS.

You want to sneer at her, but this is the only thing the two of you have agreed upon in the past twenty-three minutes that you've been stuck together in the underworld.

You stare at the eight years younger version of yourself and try to recognize her. Her hair's longer, and for a second you stroke your slowly returning fro. She's skinnier, and you can admit you're envious; you wish you could fit back into those thighs you hated so much. But it's not the hair or the weight or the unscarred skin that makes your envy sit uncomfortably on the roof of your mouth, itching to say something mean.

You can't help but think one word: light.

Light, as in the one visible in her I-haven't-seen-year-twenty-two-yet eyes.

Light, as in the weight not present on her I-have-seen-year-fourteen-but-do-not-understand-it-yet shoulders.

Light, as in the footsteps of her I-still-think-I-will-see-year-thirty feet.

She's gross in her innocence, her simplicity, so you turn away from her too discerning eyes to figure out where you are. You take in the oak tables with the blue strip on their rim and the navy, three paneled chairs and sigh. The faint hum of outside chatter and vague smell of teenaged sweat should've been a dead giveaway.

"Geography classroom," she confirms for you. "I don't understand why, though."

You do, but she is still three years away from even beginning to realize there was a problem with year fourteen, much less understanding it was a deep enough scar that the scene of the crime is your conscious' version of hell.

"I like geography." She really does, will even consider majoring in it two years later. "Math is hell." And well, that one still tracks.

She keeps contemplating other venues that should be hell instead. You walk the four walls of the classroom and try the windows to see if they will open, but they don't. She wonders aloud if she understands biology enough to hate it and consider it hell.

She really does talk too much, but you only think that because a boy will tell her so in three years, and it resounds in your head. So, you let her speak, wishing you still had the guts to do so as effortlessly.

"I think the more pertinent question is how do we get out of here," you say.

"I wasn't really asking questions, more making observations."

"Well, observe a way out of here, then, smartass."

She sits in the seat of the crime, and you try not to scream at her to get up.

"Shouldn't we figure out why we're here in the first place?"

You remember her being like that. Always concerned with the root of something, the question behind the question.

"I'm all ears," you say, turning your back on where she's propped her feet up on the table. You try the one door again. It was the first thing you had done when you had woken up in the room. Because that is who you are now—always looking for the exit, the answer. You're not sure who is more right.

"I had a normal day. School, ballet, home. I went to sleep and woke up here. You?"

You must protect her. "I don't think I should tell you. Spoilers, y'know?"

"Well, I won't tell you anything else, then," she says, crossing her arms. You roll your eyes at your stupid competitive streak. You never knew how to be at a disadvantage, to admit weakness.

"I've lived eight years since your normal day. I remember everything." And because you can, and she won't know why, yet, you tip her shoulder. She startles, off-balanced, and stutters out of the seat. It wasn't your intention, but it is easier to see her sprawled on the floor than in that chair.

She glares up at you. That defiant, inherently teenaged jut of her chin pushing upward, as though it will make her tiny being seem bigger, occupy more space.

"Ok then, know-it-all, tell me why I'm staring at an older, more miserable version of myself?"

Whenever you've wondered what younger-you would think of older-you, you imagined she'd be excited by how far you've come. You always thought she would see the best—the degrees, the accolades, the comfortable way you wear your skin. The fact that you can down a shot of white rum and not even wince anymore. You never realized you only thought about her in regard to your achievements.

You're unprepared for her to see everything that has gone wrong; for her to size you up and criticize you the same way you criticized her as soon as you wound up in this room together.

"You're just as miserable," you say. It's weak as comebacks go, but you still haven't learned how to be at a disadvantage.

"Yeah, but I'm a teenager. What's your excuse?"

That you were once a teenager. That you no longer can be. "Misery evolves," you say instead.

She's still on the floor, now sitting in a side split. You can't help but smile at her.

"Summer's coming up, huh? You must be excited."

Her face lights up, and now you know exactly what stage of fifteen she is.

"So, it's going to go well, then," she says.

You think about the ballet summer intensive that resulted in surgery and killed any desire you had to be a professional ballerina. You think about all the doors it shut, and the million more it opened. Some of which you still haven't stumbled upon.

You laugh and say, "In a manner of speaking."

She nods, satisfied. It's important she goes into it bright eyed. Bright eyes are the only way to look at impending cliffs.

"We should get out of here," she says and holds out a hand for you to help her up. You wonder if laziness is something you will ever outgrow.

She puts her hand on the doorknob and looks at you beside her. "Do you know why the geography room?"

You should've known she was stalling for time. Talking and talking until she ran into the thing she really wanted to say.

"Yes. And you know what's funny?"

"What?"

"So do you."

She does the cute, furrowed brow that you've always liked the look of on yourself. It's weird not to see it in a mirror.

"Whatever. I'll figure it out."

You know she will and wish you could save her the pain. She twists the handle and the door swings open.

"Have you known you could open it this whole time?"

She looks back at you and smirks. "I was trying to figure it out."

You shove past her, tipping her shoulder once again.

"If you read that damn Greek myths book you were supposed to in grade seven, you'd know not to look back at someone when you're walking out of hell."

Then again, maybe that's why we're still stuck there.

TWO

Apartment 337

THE TWO OF YOU WALK OUT OF THE ROOM AND INTO ANOTHER YOU KNOW SO VERY INTIMATELY.

"What is this place?" she asks looking around.

Your stomach lurches, but the laugh rolls out of you. You run through the living room and into the bedroom where you flop onto your grey duvet.

"Fuck, I love this bed."

She's in the doorway standing uncertainly, but still the eyes— light and discerning.

"It's kinda cool to hear you curse so freely."

She looks at all the things on the wall. The sprawling blue tapestry taking up the entirety of the one behind your bed. She buys it in four years on a beach in Italy. The wall beside it is covered in yellow sticky notes placed with no real pattern or intention, just like the old photos of your parents and brothers beside them. For a minute, you're glad you don't have any recent ones hanging on the wall. There are enough spoilers in this place. Your stomach swims.

"We live here."

It's not a question. She can see the life we've injected into this place. She does a full 360, then turns to where you're now snuggled under the covers. You stick your nose into the teal sheets hoping the smell will tell you what stage of life you're supposed to be at in this place. You lived so many here in such a short space of time.

"Show me."

You sit up reluctantly. Your favorite thing was to spend days lying in this bed. Nothing to do and nowhere to go.

"Fine. But don't ask questions that you know I can't answer." Or that you won't want to.

You roll out of the bed and take her back through the small apartment to the entrance.

"Let's start with the most important thing: this is where you keep your books." You take her into the little nook beside the door and open the cupboard.

"Where exactly is here? What country? State? School? How

old are we?"

"I literally said five seconds ago: don't ask me questions that you know I can't answer."

She looks at me imploringly. "If you met thirty-year-old-you, or us, or whatever, wouldn't you want spoilers?"

You don't know if thirty-year-old-you will ever exist. "Only one."

"Then I get only one, too."

You sigh, because you walked into that trap. It makes you proud that you've always known how to back someone into a corner.

"Okay, agreed. Which one of those questions do you want me to answer?"

"None. I can wait to know all that."

"Then what's the question?"

"I'll get back to you. I have to think."

"I cannot believe I was this aggravating."

"Just keep going."

You take her to the kitchen. She marvels at all the empty wine bottles. You look at the amount of tequila left in the bottle on the counter to see if you can gauge what year you've found yourselves in. Your stomach tumbles and the level of tequila lowers.

"That wasn't there before."

You turn to where she's pointing. There's a black, green, and gold scarf with the word "Jamaica" emblazoned on it now hanging over the entrance to your bedroom. Post-it notes have now made it onto the living room wall. She walks over to read them.

"Did you write this?"

You walk to where she is, sinking your toes into the carpet. You briefly glance at the blue futon and smile fondly. You look at the post-it note. The song on it didn't come out until the fall of year twenty-one. Your stomach rumbles. It feels as though it's climbing. You look back to the scarf. You didn't get it until the summer of year twenty-one. The tequila had lowered, as though you had drunk from it. The apartment is aging. You turn your back to the kitchen counter. You know what's going to appear there next. You take her back into the bedroom.

"I only see your shoes," she says randomly. But then you think, and you get it, and in that moment, you decide not to take her into the closet. It would be painfully obvious you live here alone. That was a comfort for twenty through to twenty-two-year-old-you. She might think it sad, though. She doesn't like being alone, yet.

"Is that non-question your one question?"

"If it's a non-question then it's not a question and therefore can't be my one question."

"It's an unspoken, roundabout question, which is still a

question."

She opens a drawer before you can tell her not to. It's only your underwear.

"We live alone."

You knew she'd sound disappointed, but it still hurts to hear. Your stomach is rolling now.

"We should figure out how to get out of here. This place has too many spoilers."

And you need to get her out of here before the place ages again and the worst one pops up.

"You haven't shown me the whole place."

"It's just the bathroom, laundry, and closet through that door. Boring stuff."

"I wanna see."

You don't think there's anything much incriminating in there, and considering you've walked through every other door in this place, maybe one of the ones in there will open and get you the hell out of here. Why does this place always go from the biggest comfort to—

The humidifier has appeared in the corner of your bedroom.

No.

Your stomach heaves. You run.

She startles behind you shouting what's wrong, but you don't have time to comfort her when everything that's in you is coming back out. You only just manage to get the toilet seat up when the first wave hits. Of course, you look at it.

"Ew, is that bacon?" And of course, she does too.

Bacon means it's around the third cycle.

"We don't like bacon! This is what you get. And since when do we throw up. I can't tell the last time I've done it."

She'll break her eleven-year streak of never throwing up when she gets blackout drunk for the first time in two years. As of right now, she still doesn't drink. You wish you could tell her how drastically that will change.

Another wave comes, and now it's getting harder to breathe.

"Go into the bedroom and don't come back until you see black imprints of work boots on the carpet."

"Why? What does that mean? What's happening?"

God, she is so annoying. "Just fucking do it."

She goes. You turn to look at the sink and watch all the hair that was once on twenty-two-year-old-you's head appear in a huge mass. It disappears. You had asked your dad to get rid of it, after the two of you stared at it, dazed. He ended up throwing it in the kitchen garbage, then he took a scissors to the few strands that still desperately clung to your head. You took a shower afterward, marveled at how hot water felt on a bare scalp.

Your vision is starting to swim, which means the lightheadedness will be next. You don't want to feel what comes after that: the thing that had terrified you when this had happened in year twenty-two. But this apartment is a tomb of your worst hits, and so your heart starts beating faster than you have ever felt. As though it's trying to get a lifetime of beats into its final minutes.

"I see them—whoa, who are you?"

She follows two firefighters and paramedics into the bathroom. They are faceless and don't speak, but they calmly and efficiently load you onto a stretcher. She doesn't speak. You never do when you shut down emotionally.

"Like I said," you rasp out, breath pungent and smelling slightly of pizza. You never did get to finish your slice before they carted you out that day. "Spoilers."

The firefighters hike you up and take you back through the apartment.

You look at the blue futon and remember the boy. Head on his knee, his arm around your waist, and the TV playing lightly in the background. You remember him turning it off, picking you up, and placing you on the kitchen counter. You lay back and looked at the ceiling, mouth parted.

The firefighters take you through the front door, but you take one last look. Despite everything, you still miss this place.

The kitchen counter is littered with pill bottles, blood test order forms, medical bills, and slides of your tumor.

She picks up one of the pill bottles and walks out behind you.

THREE

Flight LX 1680

THE FIREFIGHTERS TRANSFER YOU FROM THE STRETCHER TO A SEAT ON A PLANE. They strap you in and leave. She sits beside you in the opposite aisle. You hope this imaginary plane comes with imaginary flight attendants because you could really use a drink of water to wash out the bile in your mouth. She rotates the pill bottle. The shake resounds through the empty plane.

"Welcome to Flight LX 1680. Please prepare for takeoff," a disembodied voice says.

You both brace.

Neither of you speak until you've reached cruising altitude and can unclench your jaw and release your death grip on the seat handles.

"We still don't like flying," she notes.

"We never will. Though—" You cut yourself off. Skydiving will be a fun adventure for her to discover. You smile with your secret.

"Spoilers?"

"Fun ones this time."

"Yeah, last one wasn't so fun." She shakes the pill bottle. "I know what my one question is."

"Don't ask it."

But even if she doesn't ask, she will still know. Not the particulars. Not the tumor, the surgery, the endless wait. Not the diagnosis, the stage, the treatment. Not the twelve weeks of putting poison into your system to take poison out. Not the scars it left, mentally and physically. Not the one question you want to ask the thirty-year-old version of the both of you.

If she ever manages to exist.

"I don't think I even need to." She holds up the pill bottle like an accusation. "You tried to kill yourself—us."

Your eyes have gotten worse since you were fifteen, but you still manage to read from the short distance that she has picked up the bottle of antidepressants. You groan.

"If I'm taking antidepressants, shouldn't that make me not want to kill myself?"

"The bottle is full! So clearly they're not working because you haven't taken them!"

It's true you hadn't. But depression is a side effect of dying, so year-twenty-two-you erroneously thought it would go away when you stopped dying. It didn't occur to her that she would just be going from actively dying with cancer, to passively dying by nature of living like the rest of the world. The depression lingers.

"I didn't try to kill us, dumb dumb. I know it's hard, but try and use your brain cells."

It has always been so easy to insult this version of yourself.

"Don't denigrate me!"

"Big word. I didn't know we knew that one at fifteen."

She throws the bottle at my head and misses.

"No aim. That tracks."

"You're mean," she sneers. "I can't believe I have to grow into you."

"Yeah, well, I'm still living with the fact that I was you. So I guess we hate ourself at all ages."

You've been wondering since you both popped up in hell why you were the ages you were. Why fifteen and twenty-three? She isn't even the part of fifteen where all the big things happen. But maybe that's why. This might be the last version of you that exists before you realized how bad things could get. Again, you think of the word light. You hate her ease.

Without warning, the plane nose dives.

"Look what you did!" she screams.

"Suddenly I control whatever plane of existence we're on?"

The both of you smile a bit at the double entendre. You're both braced against the seat in front of you. You think about reaching out for her hand. Despite everything, aren't you supposed to protect her?

Still, the plane crashes.

FOUR

The Gold Room Where Everyone Finally Gets What They Want

THE TWO OF YOU SIT IN THE WRECKAGE AT THE END OF A BRIDGE. You stare up at a blue, blue sky and take her hand. You are never gentle with the fifteen-year-old-you inside your head, but she stands before you now, and you can see the lightness in her eyes dimming and the heaviness you feel like an ever-present shroud surrounding her. You try to handle her with care you have never given any version of yourself, least of all her.

"We're okay," you say.

You're not sure it's true. But it's what you tell yourself when you've been on the floor of your shower for half an hour wondering what you're trying to get clean from. What is within you that must be burned out. You hold the words like a litany of prayer.

"You have tattoos," she says, wiping her tears. She is looking at your feet. It occurs to you that your body has been a spoiler this entire time, as she gently runs a finger down the ink by your scar. She'll get that scar in just a few months, after the summer intensive goes awry. It'll take a few more years for it to become special to her. And the others? Well, they're stories.

"What do they mean?" she asks, but then she catches herself. "Don't answer. I'll find out soon."

She lifts your clasped hands and helps you up this time. You're breathing normally now. You look down at your legs, feeling the regained strength of year twenty-three. You keep holding her hand as you walk along the cobblestone bridge.

"Well, I don't know this place, but I guess you do," she says.

"Actually, I have no idea where we are."

You reach the middle of the bridge and look below. It's a normal river moving slowly. Beyond it are mountains you will never reach and, bizarrely, a beach. It's as though the scenery is a hotchpotch of landscapes you should recognize.

"There's a pink dress and a book. That mean anything?"

"It's coral," you say automatically, without even looking toward it.

She looks at you perplexedly.

"The color is coral, not pink," you explain.

"That's unnecessarily specific." And you know she is arguing just to argue because it is something you both do so well.

"It's a specification that will mean a lot to you one day."

You pick up the dress and hold it out in front of you. You only wore this dress once, ending that night on a bridge with a smile tucked into the corner of your mouth, and eyes for a boy who was such a revelation back then. For years you forgot about that dress and that moment, until your pain ridden body lay in a bed desperate for relief and brought you back to it. This bright spot of coral in the middle of the greyest days of your life.

You pick up the book, because maybe you do know where you are after all.

All the pages are blank except for the last one, but even so, you know what book it is. You know what will be written.

> *We were in the gold room*
> *where everyone finally gets what they want.*

You show it to her because technically the book is already published, even if you haven't discovered it at fifteen.

"We're not in a room. And it's not very gold."

"Use those literature skills li'l miss."

You know that by now English has become her favorite

subject and that she is thinking of where it can take her.

"We've always loved mountains. We definitely love the beach. Not sure about bridges and rivers. Or what the dress means."

"The dress is a moment where you had something you didn't even know you wanted."

You think of the tattoo you got weeks after it. Your first one. *Eudaimonia*.

"And the bridge?"

You shrug. "Scene of the crime."

She side-eyes you. "You're answering my questions."

"Always so suspicious when you get what you want," you laugh.

You put the dress back on the ledge and then stand on it.

"Don't jump!"

And you cringe that that is her first thought. Maybe you were looking for exits even back then.

"We're not jumping. Come on."

You climb over, onto the triangle ledge that, though you hadn't looked, you knew would be there. She hesitates, making sure to look, but she joins you.

"One day, I hope we learn to jump without looking," you say.

"You said we weren't jumping," she counters.

"And yet you still had to look."

You sit there existing for a few minutes. This is the first place you've reached where you haven't immediately thought of finding the exit.

"I don't want to tell you why the geography room. I don't want to tell you what happened in the apartment. I don't want you to know any of it, and I wish to God you weren't going to experience it," you tell her.

She looks over at you, and the boy was right—you do have the most expressive eyes.

"Geography's one of my favorite classes because I get to sit beside him," she says.

And maybe you always knew. Isn't that the most painful thing to realize all these years later? That you knew, but you made the excuses. You protected him instead of yourself. And in a way, you always will. Because even now, you cannot warn her. And in not doing so, she hears the warning. And still, she will ignore it. And still, you will be glad she does. And still, we walk into hell willingly, stubbornly. Maybe one day, we will walk out of it empty-handed and thankful.

"Shit happens, but I make it to twenty-three," she says.

You remember a point at fifteen when you thought you wouldn't, for so many reasons that all seem so trivial now, after what you've endured. But they were so critical to her then; so big that they felt like life and death. You are still learning to respect the limited scope she had.

"Think you can curse on me now?" And there goes the cheeky smile your mother gave you. "You make it through fifteen, and every year after. And despite how it all looks, you really do have fun along the way. You kiss some boys, make some art, and go places you never would've dreamed. Do things you didn't think you had in you."

"Kiss some boys?" And the lightness returns.

You roll your eyes. "That's what you focus on? You're gonna kiss a couple of the wrong ones, so don't get too excited."

She shrugs. "Do you write about it?"

Boy do you ever.

She looks out at the mountain. The top of which you can imagine, but cannot see.

"Are you happy?" She asks.

"Not every day. And there are some periods where it feels like I never am." She will find herself in one of those periods before year fifteen is up. "But there'll be this really big red and grey tree one day. And a blue couch. And oh! A black one too, that you didn't really like at first, but you end up spending a lot of time on it with your best friends. And there'll be this TV show that you can't stop talking about. And one day, you'll sit on a bridge with this wonder of a boy that makes you think of fireflies, and he'll tip your shoulder until you look at him. He'll smile, and you'll be amazed how long it keeps you warm."

"I've never seen a firefly."

"Neither have I." And you look at her and hope she understands. Hope it will be the one thing she remembers from this dreamwalk. Hope when the time comes she will revel in the moment deeper and longer than you had. Hope she will recognize it for the marvel that it is.

You nod to the beach in the distance. "There'll be a beach that'll take some time to discover, but when you do, you'll want to spend every waking moment there because you can always feel the sun on your face. And you'll end up liking bacon as a weird side effect. And then there will be so many other foods you never thought you'd try. And you're going to dance."

"I'm going to dance?" And she's hopeful that it will be in the way she wants. And it won't be, but it'll be in the way she needs.

"You're going to *dance*. And it's going to feel brand new and like a reckoning in your soul. And you're going to find the words one day. All of them, in the right order. All those faraway places in your head, and people who will never exist, and the tangled web of worlds you run away to will come alive." You don't know that for sure, yet, but you're willing to believe it's true.

"And you're going to make so many damn mistakes that'll make your jaw clench and your hands shake, and you're going to learn from some of them, and keep returning to others until you can't anymore."

"Do we fall in love?" She whispers. And your heart aches because you have always been so desperate to be ruined by it.

"Not yet, maybe not ever. At least not in the way you're talking about. But there will come a time when you learn to measure love in the breaths in between. In the indefinable spaces you cannot hold. And you'll find you're so full to the brim of them."

She marinates in what you've said for a few minutes. Enough for you to tip your head back to the sun and be grateful it still shines on you sometimes.

"I know you say we're going to be okay, but I'm still scared that I have to go through everything. You have a lot of scars," she says.

And you don't know what to say to that. Because there are no comforting words that will assuage the hell of chemo in year-twenty-two. There is no way to prepare her for the hours of therapy when she realizes that friendship from year-fourteen wasn't the healthiest. And you yourself still haven't figured out how to deal with the constant anxiety of hoping you are around to see year-thirty, and thirty-five, and maybe sixty, and maybe so many that life feels as if it has been lived in full. You look to the beginning of the bridge, hoping to see a shadow of the eldest you. Hoping she has done it all. Made the mistakes, learned from them, and made some new ones. You hope she is happy.

"That was your one question, wasn't it? You hoped I was happy."

You touch the inked word on your foot. *Eudaimonia*. She looks at you desperately.

"I can wait to experience the details. I just want to know they're worth it."

You take in the landscape—the gold room. A beach, a mountain, a coral dress, and the version of yourself you always forget to love.

You stand and climb back on to the bridge. She scrambles up to follow you. There is so much you could tell her. But can't she see? Can't you? We make it to the gold room if we take a step forward. You take her hand again and walk to the beginning of the bridge.

"Here's a good spoiler: you become best friends with your parents."

"Really?" And you are happy to note that makes her excited and not incredulous.

"You have weekly date nights. Mum sometimes drinks rum."

"You're kidding!"

"No joke. And dad always has the best suss..."

FIVE

The Womb

YOU WALK UNTIL THE SUN LOWERS AND THE SIDES PINCH IN. The space has condensed so much that the two of you cuddle close together, unaware and uncaring of where you are.

You stare into your eyes. Hold your smaller hands. Match knobby, scarred knees together. You both look up when you hear a voice.

"She's moving so much today."

And you both smile, because you will always recognize your mother's voice.

You see the silhouette of a hand above you.

"She's a dancer," your father says.

"And she'll be more."

More. It is all you've ever wanted. All you've ever wanted to be.

You look at her. Eyes so light.

You look at her until you can see she is more. Eyes dancing with all the selves you've been, and all you've yet to be. You curl into her and breathe, listening as a soft, quick patter resounds as one.

About the Author

MARIANA SAMUDA IS FROM JAMAICA. She is a graduate of Chapman University's MFA program. She has previously published work in *Atticus Review*, *Moko Magazine*, *Headway Quarterly*, and *Hoot Review*.